ROMANS

Reading Ladder

Contents

Introduction

Let's travel back in time to ancient Rome
and discover its huge empire, rough
and tough army, homes, schools, baths,
feasts and much, much more!

Ancient Rome

Rome was built on seven hills beside the Tiber river, possibly as early as 753BCE. Let's discover some of the main attractions.

Trajan's Roman Forum was a meeting place where people discussed trade and gossiped.

Chariot races were held in the Circus Maximus. It could seat over 150,000 race fans.

The Trajan Baths could hold up to 10,000 bathers.

The Colosseum was a giant stadium where **gladiator** fights took place.

Gladiators

Welcome to the **amphitheatre**, where gladiators fought against each other to entertain the crowd. Each type of gladiator had different weapons.

The **retiarius** was armed with a **trident** and a net. Sometimes he also had a dagger.

The **hoplomachus** fought with a spear and a short sword or dagger.

The largest amphitheatre in Rome was the Colosseum. It seated over 50,000 people.

The **murmillo** fought with a sharp, straight sword.

The **thraex** had a short, curved sword.

The rise of Rome

The Romans had the biggest empire in the world – over 6.5 million square kilometres. This is how they built it up.

1. 220BCE
The empire started with Italy and then Sicily, Corsica and Sardinia were taken over.

2. 100BCE
Then the Romans captured parts of North Africa and Spain, as well as Portugal, Macedonia and Greece.

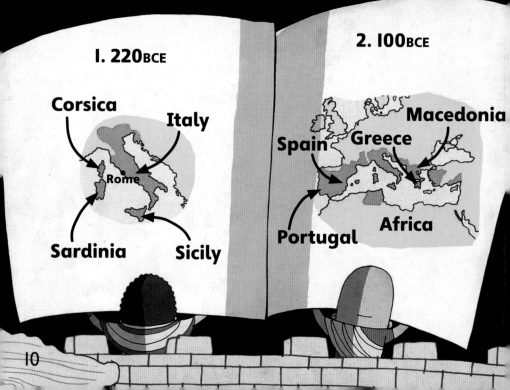

1. 220BCE

Corsica
Italy
Rome
Sardinia
Sicily

2. 100BCE

Spain
Greece
Macedonia
Portugal
Africa

3. 117–116CE

Then the Romans seized the rest of Spain, and also France, Egypt and Great Britain.

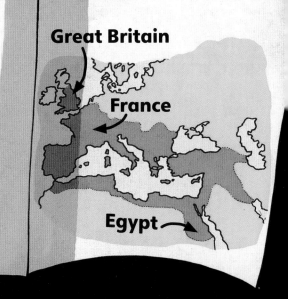

Great Britain was captured in 43CE. Emperor Hadrian built a wall across Britain to keep out the people in the north. Parts of the wall can still be seen today.

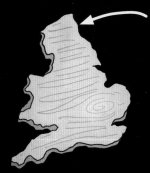

Egypt produced most of the empire's cereal and grain.

The Roman army

The Roman army was always rough and tough but a mighty makeover in 107BCE helped turn it into a fierce, fighting force.

General Gaius Marius increased the size of the Roman army. He also improved their kit and training.

A vitus (stick) for keeping soldiers under control

The centurion was in charge of about 60 to 100 legionaries (soldiers).

metal shin protector

woollen tunic

A legionary carried everything he needed in his pack, including weapons, rations and cooking utensils. It could weigh up to 30 kilograms.

sword

shield

The standard bearer carried a bronze or silver eagle.

bear skin

shield

The soldiers marched up to 40 kilometres per day!

The Celts

The Roman army fought many different enemies from Europe, the Middle East and parts of Africa. The **Celts** of Great Britain and Ireland were fierce.

The leader of one Celtic tribe was a woman called Boudicca.

The Celts covered themselves in warpaint and used long swords to scare off the Romans.

The Parthians

The **Parthians** had a large empire in western Asia.

Some Parthians fought on horseback and used a long lance or spear.

Some Parthians used bows and arrows to fight the Romans.

The Dacians

The **Dacians** came from Eastern Europe and the Romans were after their large gold mines.

Many wore a domed metal helmet.

Their sharp, curved sword was called a falx.

Their army carried a dragon-shaped banner.

The Carthaginians

The **Carthaginians** were named after the city of Carthage in North Africa. Their empire extended into Spain and the Mediterranean.

One of their generals was called Hannibal.

Hannibal's large army included some elephants!

Homes

Most Roman city-dwellers lived in a block of flats called an **insula**. The living areas were small and they didn't have a kitchen or a bathroom.

1. Cooking wasn't allowed inside because it was a fire risk.

2. It was light and airy inside as the windows didn't have any glass.

3. The flats didn't have waste pipes so any waste was thrown into gutters in the street.

4. There wasn't any running water so they collected water from the fountains and used public baths and toilets.

5. There were usually places to eat and shops on the ground floor.

19

Rich Romans lived in a house called a **domus**. This walled house didn't have any outside windows but the rooms opened out on to a courtyard and garden.

I. Rain flowed off the roof into a pool in the courtyard. This water was used for drinking or for washing.

2. The office

3. The walled garden was a peaceful retreat from the bustling city.

4. Gods were worshipped at the household shrine.

5. Slaves prepared all of the meals in the kitchen.

6. Romans ate while lying on couches in the dining room.

7. One of the bedrooms

Feasts

A feast was a treat for rich Romans. There would be 12 courses that would last for hours and hours. It certainly wasn't fast food!

Most foods were eaten using fingers. Romans rarely used knives and forks, although spoons were used for some dishes.

Musicians, acrobats and dancers entertained the guests.

Typical dishes included roasted meats and fish served with vegetables.

Baths

The Romans had their baths in public. Men and women had separate bath times.

People sweated a lot in the hottest pool.

A warm room had a small pool that contained lukewarm water.

The pools were heated by furnaces.

The Romans had no soap.
Instead they rubbed olive oil
on to their bodies and then
scraped it and the dirt off
with a blade called a strigil.

strigil

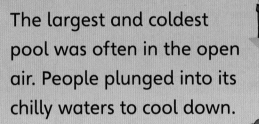

The largest and coldest
pool was often in the open
air. People plunged into its
chilly waters to cool down.

Children wrote using a wooden tool on a wooden tablet covered in a layer of wax.

tablet

School

Some Roman boys went to a primary school, called a ludus, until they were 12 years old. They were taught to read and write there. A school for children aged 13 to 16 was called a grammaticus. Let's discover more about this school.

Lessons included reading and writing
Latin and Greek, and learning
how to speak well in public. Older
children were taught about history,
geography, maths, philosophy
and astronomy.

Many children didn't go to school.
Poor children often had to work
and rich ones were usually taught
at home by a tutor. Most rich or
poor girls never went to school
and were taught at home.

Clothes

Poor Romans wore simple tunics made from rough cloth with little decoration.

A loincloth was a poor man's only underwear. It was made of rough woollen cloth, which could be really itchy!

loincloth

Poor people had to walk everywhere but they couldn't afford shoes.

Rich men wore clothes made from soft, expensive cloth and rich women wore beautiful dresses.

Rich men and women often wore jewellery, such as brooches, rings, necklaces and earrings.

Wealthy Romans wore soft leather sandals or boots. However, they usually travelled by horse or in a **litter**, so they didn't need to walk much.

Fun facts

Some feasts would have a pig stuffed with sausages and fruit. It was roasted whole and the sausages spilled out when it was cut open.

The Romans didn't have ketchup but they did have a sauce that they often poured over food. It was salty and smelly as it was made from rotting fish guts!

The school day started before sunrise and the school week lasted seven days.

Glossary

amphitheatre *(am-pea-thee-at-er)* An open-air seating area for entertainment.

BCE Before the Common Era.

Carthaginians *(Car-tha-jin-yans)* People from the city of Carthage, in Tunisia.

CE The Common Era.

Celts *(Kelts)* People who lived in Europe.

chariot *(cha-ree-ot)* A cart pulled by horses.

Dacians *(Day-shee-ans)* People who lived in Dacia (in Eastern Europe).

domus *(dough-mus)* A house for rich Romans.

gladiator *(glad-ee-ate-or)* A person trained to fight other gladiators.

hoplomachus (hop-low-mak-us) A type of gladiator.

litter A box for rich Romans to travel in.

insula *(in-shoe-la)* A flat for poor Romans.

murmillo *(mur-mill-o)* A type of gladiator.

Parthians *(Par-thee-ans)* People from Parthia in Iran.

retiarius *(ret-ee-ar-e-us)* A type of gladiator.

thraex *(tray-ex)* A type of gladiator.

trident *(try-dent)* A spear with three points.

Index